I, *Geronimo Stilton*, have a lot of mouse friends, but none as **spooky** as my friend CREEPELLA VON CACKLEFUR! She is an enchanting and MYSTERIOUS mouse with a pet bat named **Bitewing**. Creepella lives in a **CEMETERY**, sleeps in a marble **sarcophagus**, and drives a **hearse**. By night she is a special effects and set designer for SCARY FILMS, and by day she's studying to become a journalist! Her father, Boris von Cacklefur, runs the funeral home Fabumouse Funerals, and the von Cacklefur family owns the **CREEPY** Cacklefur Castle, which sits on top of a skull-shaped mountain in MYSTERIOUS VALLEY.

YIKES! I'm a real 'fraidy mouse, but even I think Creepella and her family are AWFULLY fascinating. I can't wait for you to read this fa-mouse-ly funny and SPECTACULARLY SPOOKY tale!

Geronimo Stilton

Creepella von Cacklefur

Bitewing

Billy Squeakspeare

Grandpa Frankenstein

A journalist who lives in Mysterious Valley and solves spooky cases with her inseparable pet bat, Bitewing.

A famous writer and friend of Creepella.

An extremely mad scientist and an expert in Egyptian mummies.

Snip and Snap

Shivereen

Grandma Crypt

Troublemaking twins and expert spies.

Dolores

Kafka

Creepella's favorite niece.

She loves spiders, and her pet is a gigantic tarantula named Dolores.

The von Cacklefur family's pet cockroach.

Booey the Poltergeist

The mischievous ghost who haunts Cacklefur Castle.

Boneham

The butler to the von Cacklefur family, and a snob right down to the tips of his whiskers.

Baby

He was adopted and raised with love by the von Cacklefurs.

Chef Stewrat

The cook at Cacklefur Castle. He dreams of creating the ultimate stew.

Boris von Cacklefur

Creepella's father, and the funeral director at Fabumouse Funerals.

Madame LaTomb

The family housekeeper. A ferocious were-canary nests in her hair.

Chompers

The von Cacklefur family's meat-eating guard plant.

Geronimo Stilton

CREEPELLA VON CACKLEFUR

A SUITCASE FULL OF GHOSTS

Scholastic Inc.

ISBN 978-0-545-74611-3

Copyright © 2011 Edizioni Piemme S.p.A., Corso Como 15, 20154 Milan, Italy.

International Rights © Atlantyca S.p.A.

English translation © 2015 by Atlantyca S.p.A.

GERONIMO STILTON names, characters, and related indicia are copyright, trademark, and exclusive license of Atlantyca S.p.A. All rights reserved. The moral right of the author has been asserted.

Based on an original idea by Elisabetta Dami.
www.geronimostilton.com

Published by Scholastic Inc., 557 Broadway, New York, NY 10012. SCHOLASTIC and associated logos are trademarks and/or registered trademarks of Scholastic Inc.

Stilton is the name of a famous English cheese. It is a registered trademark of the Stilton Cheese Makers' Association. For more information, go to www.stiltoncheese.com.

Text by Geronimo Stilton
Original title *Una valigia piena di fantasmi*
Cover by Giuseppe Ferrario (pencils and inks) and
Giulia Zaffaroni (color)
Illustrations by Ivan Bigarella (pencils and inks) and
Daria Cerchi (color)
Graphics by Yuko Egusa

Special thanks to Tracey West
Translated by Andrea Schaffer
Interior design by Becky James

12 11 10 9 8 7 6 5 4 3 2 1   15 16 17 18 19 20/0

Printed in the U.S.A.   40

First printing, August 2015

A Surprise
from the Sky

It was a very **HOT** day, hot enough to make a **GRILLED CHEESE** sandwich on the sidewalk. But I didn't mind, even though I was stuck in a very **L O N G** line with my nephew, Benjamin. It was worth it. Want to know why?

First, let me introduce myself! My name is Stilton, *Geronimo Stilton*, and I run *The Rodent's Gazette*, the most famouse newspaper on Mouse Island.

And now, let me tell you why I was waiting in line with **BENJAMIN** on that **sunny** afternoon.

You see, the **FLYING FUR CIRCUS**

was in town! Every rodent in New Mouse City wanted to see the show. It featured magicians, cheese jugglers, and expert acrobats. Benjamin was so **excited** that his whiskers were twitching!

"Uncle, what's that up there?" he exclaimed suddenly, pointing.

Look at that!

Upsy-daisy!

I saw a **dark** spot in the bright blue sky. "Maybe it's a cloud," I guessed. "A little bit of rain would cool down my fur nicely. But . . . it's moving so *quickly*. It looks like it's coming right toward us!"

"Uncle, **DUCK**!" Benjamin yelled.

But his warning came too late.

Something fell right on my head!

BAM!

"That's not a cloud, Uncle. It's a bat!" Benjamin informed me.

Massaging my skull, I looked up. I recognized that bat flying above me. It was **Bitewing**, the pet of the spooky von Cacklefur family.

"Ha! Nice catch, Clumsy Paws!"

I picked up what the bat had dropped on me: a purple **notebook** with the initials of my friend Creepella on the cover.

"It's a new book! Publish it RIGHT AWAY!" Bitewing squeaked.

"Read it out loud now!" pleaded Benjamin, who loved Creepella's thrilling stories.

He didn't have to ask me twice. You see,

I have joined Creepella on many of her adventures. They are always full of **CREEPY** characters, **MYSTERIOUS** happenings, and settings as **GLOOMY** as moldy cheese. I was curious to discover which tale she had decided to tell this time. I opened the **notebook**, cleared my throat, and began to read aloud . . .

Let's see . . .

I'm sure it's another thrilling tale!

A SUITCASE FULL OF GHOSTS

TEXT AND ILLUSTRATIONS BY
CREEPELLA VON CACKLEFUR

A Mysterious Stranger

Darkness had fallen over Mysterious Valley. A **stranger** walked through the streets of Gloomeria. Only the rays of the moon, as PALE as mozzarella, lit his way.

Then clouds covered the **MOON**, and the curious rodent stopped, lost.

"I'm more tired than a sleepless ghost!" he muttered sadly. "I'm afraid I took a wrong turn a while back, and now I have no idea where my PAWS are taking me."

With a sigh, he set down the enormouse suitcase that he was dragging with him.

"I should stop here," he reasoned. "I can

start my journey again at dawn. Now I just need a safe place to rest . . ."

But where? Empty fields surrounded him. In the distance he could see the silhouette of a GHOSTLY castle, but it was very far, and he was very tired.

Suddenly, a lone ray of MOONLIGHT managed to squeeze through the clouds and light up a bare WALNUT tree.

"What a bizarre-looking tree!"

he thought aloud. "But it's just what I need. I can rest against its nice, wide trunk."

And so the traveler dragged his suitcase to the tree and propped it up next to him. Then he leaned against the trunk and fell immediately into a deep sleep.

Of course, he never imagined that he would

soon be **disturbed** by the most bothersome twins in all of Mysterious Valley . . .

TROUBLESOME TWINS

"Hurry up, **SNIP**!"

"I'm coming, **SNAP**!"

The terrible von Cacklefur twins came **tiptoeing** down the stairs of Cacklefur Castle. They had woken up extra early to perform their latest mission, **PERFECT PRANK NUMBER 7,458:** Stealing the Sweet Stew Leftovers from Yesterday's Dinner.

All they had to do was get to the kitchen before the rest of the family woke up, **steal** the stew, and then go back to their room to gobble it up.

It was a perfect, simple plan. But even simple plans can go wrong. The twins were opening up the refrigerator when they heard a **BOOMING** voice.

"WHAT ARE YOU TWO UP TO?"

It was Chef Stewrat, the cook of the von Cacklefur castle. He had woken up early, too, to fetch a nice **moldy** radish from the garden. Poor Madame LaTomb had an awful **COLD**, and he wanted to make her his special Feel Better Stew.

"**STOP** right there, you plucky pests!" he yelled, waving his ladle.

Snip and Snap scampered out of the

kitchen in a *flash*, chased by Chef Stewrat.

"If I catch you I will **MUMMIFY** you!" he yelled.

But the twins were way ahead of him. They didn't stop until the chef's voice was an echo far behind them.

"How . . . PUFF . . . far . . . PANT . . . have we gone, Snip?" Snap asked.

Stop right there!

"Far . . . **PANT** . . . enough. We're at the walnut tree!" Snip replied.

The pale moon lit up a strange sight in front of the twins.

"Look, Snip!" cried Snap. "There's a rodent sleeping here."

Try to catch us!

Run, Snap!

"And he's **snoring** like an embalmed mummy," Snip said.

"And he's got a very big **SUITCASE**," added Snap.

The twins should have known not to open the suitcase. But their curiosity got the better of them. It opened with a **CLICK!** On the inside there were a lot of jars. Snip and Snap pulled some out and read the labels.

TUMBLING GHS.

JUGGLING PHS.

MAGICIAN ECTO.

"What are they, Snap?" Snip asked.

"I have **no idea**, Snip," Snap admitted.

"But I think we should borrow this jar."

Snap pointed to a jar labeled:

PRANKSTER
GHS.

"I don't know what 'GHS' stands for, but I like the pranking part," said Snip, grabbing the jar.

The twins closed the suitcase and walked away, laughing.

Not too long after, the first rays of sunlight hit the stranger's snout. He woke up, yawning.

"Time to get back on the ROAD," he said.

He got up, smoothed his crumpled jacket, and continued his journey.

STRANGER THAN USUAL

The rays of sunlight grew **STRONGER**, pushing their way through the heavy **purple** curtains of Creepella von Cacklefur's bedroom.

"Hurry up! Hurry up! Hurry up!" screeched Bitewing.

Creepella had stayed up very late the night before, working on a research paper. As a result, she had slept a little bit later than usual.

But the research was finished (for a scholarly paper titled *The Midnight Dreams of Mummies*), and Creepella had been

looking forward to a *leisurely* morning. She was consulting with Wardrobe, her talking closet, trying to find the perfect outfit.

Until Bitewing interrupted her.

"I said, **hurry**! Aren't you listening?" Bitewing squeaked.

"Quit making such a *racket*," Creepella scolded. "What's so important?"

"Well, Madame LaTomb has a dreadful cold, but that's not the worst thing," Bitewing replied. "Those **terrible twins** are up to their old tricks! They replaced all my candied crickets with colored **BUTTONS**! Yuck!"

Creepella laughed. "It's up to Boneham to keep those two in line," she said.

"Boneham! That **BONY**

butler can't control those twins," Bitewing complained.

"Well, it's not my problem," Creepella replied. "I FINISHED my research. I'm not teaching a class at the Shivery Arts Academy today. I don't even have an article due for *The Shivery News*! I want to enjoy a **day of Laziness**, starting with a nice walk. What do you say, **KAFKA**?"

She looked over at the foot of her bed, where Kafka, her giant pet **cockroach**, slept. But he wasn't there!

"Kafka, where are you?" Creepella called out, crouching to check under the bed. Then she **shook** a box of Critter Crispies — licorice-flavored treats for cockroaches. Kafka loved them. But even this did not make him appear.

"This is strange," Creepella said. "Let's go look for him, Bitewing!"

As she headed down the stairs, Creepella almost ran into Grandma Crypt, who was **frantically** running *up* the stairs.

"Grandma! What happened?" Creepella asked.

"My NEEDLES! My NEEDLES!" she replied.

Creepella was confused. "Your needles?"

"My knitting needles," Grandma Crypt explained. "I can't find them, and I need to finish the leg warmers I am making for my TARANTULAS. That's a lot of legs to knit for, you know."

Creepella frowned. "I'll bet it was SNiP and SnaP. I suppose I'll have to LOOK for them after all."

On the first floor she met Shivereen, her niece, who was distraught.

"Auntie Creepella, look!" she cried, holding out her school notebooks. All of the pages had been glued together with some mysterious SLIMY substance!

Before Creepella could comment, Boris von Cacklefur appeared at the door, holding something between his PAWS.

"Rattle my bones! If I ever discover who did this —"

How bizarre . . . .

Look, Auntie!

"What happened, Daddy?" Creepella asked.

"Look at this EXTREMELY VALUABLE Supercomfy Coffin I have to deliver this morning," her father replied. "Someone jabbed knitting needles right through the bottom of it!"

"**KNITTING NEEDLES?** Let me see," said Grandma Crypt, walking up to him. "Yes, those are **mine**. But how did they wind up there?"

Creepella frowned. "This time Snip and Snap have really gone **too far**! They need a good talking-to. But where are they?"

A Curious Cockroach

Creepella and Shivereen inspected Cacklefur Castle ROOM BY ROOM, looking for the twins. They began with the top floor, examining *Madame LaTomb's* chamber. They found the housekeeper still under the covers, with a heap of lace handkerchiefs **crumpled** on the nightstand.

"Good morning, Miss Cree — ACHOO! — pella. Is everything — ACHOO! — okay?" she asked between sneezes.

Aaa · · ·

· · ·choo!

With every sneeze, Howler, the were-canary that lives in her hair, quietly echoed with another sneeze: "**ACHOO!**"

"I'm sorry you're sick, Madame," said Creepella. "I am looking for the **twins**. Have you seen them, by any chance?"

"No, dear. I — **ACHOO!** — was asleep until a few minutes ago," she answered. "What have they duh — duh — **ACHOO!** — done now?"

"What haven't they done?!" replied Creepella. "They've really gone **wild** today! But I'll keep looking for them. I hope you feel better."

As she turned to leave, Shivereen let out a **SHRIEK**.

"Auntie, look!" she cried, pointing at Madame LaTomb's collection of dolls.

"The **dolls**? Yes, I've seen them — they're beautiful," said Creepella.

"Yes, but don't you notice anything strange?" her niece asked.

The pretty little dolls all wore fancy dresses and polished shoes. And in the middle of them was a male wearing a vest with BLUE AND WHITE sailor stripes. But that was no little sailor doll — it was a live cockroach!

"Kafka! Who dressed you like this?" Shivereen asked, picking up the pet cockroach.

"IT'S THOSE TWINS AGAIN!" Creepella fumed. "When I find those two, I'll put them in the basement to **mold** with the aged cheese!"

She stormed out of the room, eager to find the twins. Shivereen followed her. Bitewing flew up to Creepella as she walked down the stairs.

"Here you are!" he squeaked. "Where were you? You left your phone in your room! It's been ringing and ringing!"

He dropped the cell phone into Creepella's paws.

Here you are!

The **BOOMING** voice of Edward Squeaker, the editor in chief of *The Shivery News*, exploded from the phone.

"Creepella! We need an exclusive interview with

Hector Spector. And if you want to write again for our paper, it'll be on my desk tomorrow morning at seven, and not a **millisecond** later!"

"Who is this Hector?" Creepella asked, but she got no answer. The grouchy editor had already **hung up** on her!

A Lucky Meeting

"I guess the hunt for those rascal twins will have to wait," Creepella said. "Now I have to go on a mission to find and interview a rodent named Hector Spector."

"Who is he?" asked Shivereen.

"I don't know, but I think I've heard the name Hector Spector before," Creepella said thoughtfully.

Just then, Grandpa Frankenstein passed by with his 🐾🐾🐾🐾 full of test tubes.

"Hector Spector? Did you say Hector Spector?" he asked excitedly.

Creepella was **astonished**. "Do you

know him?"

"Of course! He is without a doubt the greatest!" replied Grandpa.

"The greatest what?" asked Creepella.

"The best!" Grandpa said.

"The best what?" asked Creepella.

"He's the most amazing —"

"Just tell us who he is!" yelled Shivereen, frustrated.

Who?

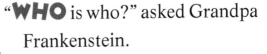

"WHO is who?" asked Grandpa Frankenstein.

Creepella sighed. Her grandfather's BRILLIANT mind often wandered.

"Hector Spector," she reminded him.

"Ah, yes, him!" Grandpa cried. "He is the owner of the GALLOPING GHOST

CIRCUS. Why, is it in town?"

"It must be, if Squeaker wants me to interview him," Creepella replied.

Grandpa grinned. "Wonderful! When you see him, please get me a **TICKET** to the show. It is the most **gorgeously ghastly** show I have ever seen!"

Grandpa Frankenstein tottered off. Shivereen looked up at her aunt.

"Auntie, can I come with you?" she asked. "This circus of ghosts seems **SCARY** enough to make my **fur** stand on end!"

"Of course," Creepella replied. "But first, we need to get *Geronimo*. He is a great journalist, and he will lend me a paw with the interview. Then we'll try to figure out where Hector is staying."

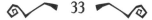

Minutes later, they were *zooming* down the street in the **Turborapid 3000**. They hadn't gone far when Shivereen exclaimed, "LOOK! There's someone walking on the side of the road."

In fact, a rodent wearing *elegant* but *wrinkled* clothes was trudging along the road, dragging a heavy suitcase.

"He seems to be having a **hard time**,"

Who is that?

Creepella mused. She slowed down and called out to the traveler. "Hello, sir! Can we **help** you in some way?"

The rodent turned his head. He looked **exhausted**. "Thank you so much! That is very kind of you," he said. "If it isn't too much **trouble**, may I ask you for a ride to my hotel?"

"Of course!" Creepella answered.

Oof . . .

Creepella pulled over and opened the door for the TRAVELER.

"Nice to meet you," she said. "My name is Creepella, and this is my niece, Shivereen."

"You both are very **kind**," the rodent repeated as he got in the car. "Let me introduce myself as well. My name is Hector Spector!"

A GHOSTLY HOTEL

"Hector Spector!" exclaimed Creepella. "Is it really you?"

"In the fur and whiskers!"

he responded proudly. "Have you heard of me before?"

"Yes! You are the owner of the GALLOPING GHOST CIRCUS!" Shivereen piped up.

"Hee, hee! That's me! My circus is like no other," he bragged, handing Shivereen his business card. "I'm certain you would love it!"

HECTOR SPECTOR

Owner of the spookiest circus in the world!
Our shows will frighten you with juggling phantoms,
tumbling ectoplasm, and acrobatic ghosts.
If we don't scare you out of your fur,
we'll refund your money!

"I am a reporter for *The Shivery News*, the most **famouse** daily newspaper in Mysterious Valley," explained Creepella. "And I must interview you!"

"I would be very **happy** to do an interview," Hector replied. "But first, I would like to rest at the hotel I have been **LOOKING** for all night. The owner sent me a map with directions, but I'm afraid I got lost."

"Of course!" Creepella agreed. "Shivereen, can you please look at the map and see where it is?"

Hector gave the map to Shivereen, and she studied it carefully.

"So **where** should I go?" Creepella asked her.

"It's funny, but if I'm not mistaken, the **HOTEL** is actually the Rattenbaum Mansion," Shivereen told her.

Creepella **SLAMMED** on the brakes. "What? Let me see."

Humble home of the very mean von Cacklefur family

Very luxurious hotel of the noble Rattenbaum family

Our walnut tree!

The Rattenbaums were very unpleasant neighbors, always causing trouble. What were they up to now?

"Hmm, I didn't know they had transformed their mansion into a hotel," she said thoughtfully. "When did Shamley do that?"

Creepella put the car back into GEAR and drove to the Rattenbaum Mansion. Soon they arrived at the battered garden GATE. Someone had posted a shaky sign there.

"**GRAND HOTEL?**" Creepella read out loud. "We'll see about that."

"Are you sure this is the place?" Hector asked, looking at the peeling paint *Um . . .* and *FALLING* shingles on the face of the old mansion.

"Don't worry, I'll come inside with you," Creepella told him. "Shivereen, please wait in the car!"

She **knocked** on the door, but no one opened it. She gently pushed it open, and it let out a loud creak. A feeble candle lit up the hallway.

"Is anyone here? I brought Mr. Spector!" Creepella called out **LOUDLY**.

"Mr. Spector? **Welcome**, our honored guest!"

The booming voice belonged to Shamley

Rattenbaum. He stood at the top of the stairs, rudely yelling down at Creepella and Hector.

"Don't just stand there until your tail gets moldy, Mr. Spector. Make yourself at home! Make yourself at home!" Then he squinted. "Is that one of the detestable VON CACKLEFURS with you?"

"Don't worry about me, I'm just leaving!" Creepella yelled back at him. She did not want to stay in that musty mansion for another second. But as she turned to leave, she heard a familiar voice.

"My name is Stilton, *Geronimo Stilton*! It isn't *Squilton*!"

SOME CHEESY POETRY

Creepella froze for a second, standing as still as a MUMMY. Then she hurried toward the Rattenbaums' dusty living room.

"Geronimo Stilton! What are YOU doing here?" she exclaimed in SURPRISE.

Geronimo was sitting around a rickety table surrounded by the female members of the Rattenbaum family: the three triplets — Tilly, Milly, and Lilly — and Ladi Fifi, their snooty grandmother. A tea set and a plate of cheese biscuits topped the table.

Poor Geronimo was LOOKING left and right, like he was trying to escape. His EYES

widened when he saw Creepella.

"Creepella! What are you doing here?"

"I asked you first," she said. "Shouldn't you be busy writing the *Encyclopedia of Ghosts*?"

Creepella had brought Geronimo to Gloomeria to work on the 754-volume encyclopedia.

"Well, yes, but —" Geronimo began.

"We invited him —" interrupted Milly.

"— to our big," interrupted Tilly.

"— Poetry Tea!" completed Lilly.

"And what exactly is poetic about this tea?" Creepella asked, noticing the messy cheese crumbs strewn everywhere.

Lady Fifi cleared her throat. "For your information, in my glorious youth I was not only a highly praised actor in silent films but also a celebrated author of love

poems! And Mr. *Squilton* has the honor today of hearing me recite them."

She began to recite, with her snout in the air:

"My darling, I loved you more than Cheddar! In fact, nobody loved you better!"

An embarrassed silence fell over the room. Lady Fifi took it as encouragement.

"When you left me, you broke my heart! I cried all over my cream cheese tart!"

"Tremendous!"
"Terrifying!"
"THRILLING!"

The triplets applauded.

"I didn't want to come, believe me," Geronimo whispered to Creepella. "I am only on page 1,327 of the encyclopedia! But the triplets said they would sic the Cheesy Ghost on me unless I came to the tea!"

"Honestly, Gerrykins! The Cheesy Ghost isn't even that SCARY," Creepella said. Just then, she heard a squeak and the fluttering of little wings behind her.

"Bitewing! What are YOU doing here?" she asked.

"I was looking for you and I saw the Turborapid 3000 in the garden," Bitewing replied. "What are YOU doing in Rattenbaum Mansion?"

"It's a long story,"

I didn't want to come!

Creepella said. "So what's going on?"

"Cacklefur Castle is in **upheaval**!" cried Bitewing. "You must get home!

EMERGENCY! EMERGENCY! EMERGENCYYYY!"

"Okay," Creepella said. "Gerrykins, let's get away from this **cheesy poetry**."

She grabbed him by the collar and pulled him away. The Rattenbaum triplets exchanged looks. Geronimo was the most **interesting** visitor they'd had in ages. They weren't just going to let him go!

Creepella and Geronimo **snuck** out of the mansion. Lady Fifi's snout was still in the air, so she didn't notice. She kept reciting her **poetry**.

"My tears run hot like melted cheese.
I hope your fur gets infested with fleas!"

Then she opened her eyes. "Mr.
Squilton, where are you? Mr. Squiiiiiiiiilton?"

A Not-So-Grand Hotel

Hector Spector was still standing by the front door of the Grand Hotel Rattenbaum with his enormouse **SUITCASE** at his feet. He watched as Creepella, Geronimo, and Bitewing *hurried* right past his snout. A few seconds later, the triplets followed them.

Before he could ask questions, Shamley Rattenbaum came up to him and put a paw on his shoulder. "My dear Mr. Spector! Come, let me show you the hotel!"

Shamley PROUDLY waved his paw in the hallway. "The Rattenbaums are the finest family in Mysterious Valley. My

ancestors built this mansion years ago, and now we've turned it into this fine hotel. Let me show you every **nook** and *cranny*."

Hector Spector walked right into a sticky **spiderweb**. "Could you just please show me my room? I'd like to get some rest."

Shamley looked disappointed. "Oh, okay." He led Hector through the *Gloomy Gallery*, a **HALL** decorated with portraits of the Rattenbaum ancestors. Like Lady Fifi, they all had their snouts in the air. Hector noticed **CRACKS** in the walls and more peeling paint. This place sure didn't look like a luxury hotel!

They went upstairs and turned into an even more narrow and dreary hallway. Hector noticed the old, **TORN** wallpaper and shook his head. Now he was convinced. This wasn't a hotel. It was just a **crumbling**

old house!

Shamley stopped in front of a tiny door. "Here we are!" he cried.

He opened the door to reveal a tiny room with a tiny, **rickety** canopy bed, a tiny desk half-eaten by **termites**, and a tiny wardrobe with an open door that kept swinging back and forth, **CREAKING**. The wallpaper was peeling, and there were stains everywhere.

"Is this the **luxury** suite you promised me?" Hector asked. He couldn't believe his eyes.

"**OF COURSE!** Of course! The finest in Mysterious Valley!" Shamley insisted. "Now, let me let you get some rest."

He quickly backed out of the room, **slamming** the door behind him. The whole house **shook**.

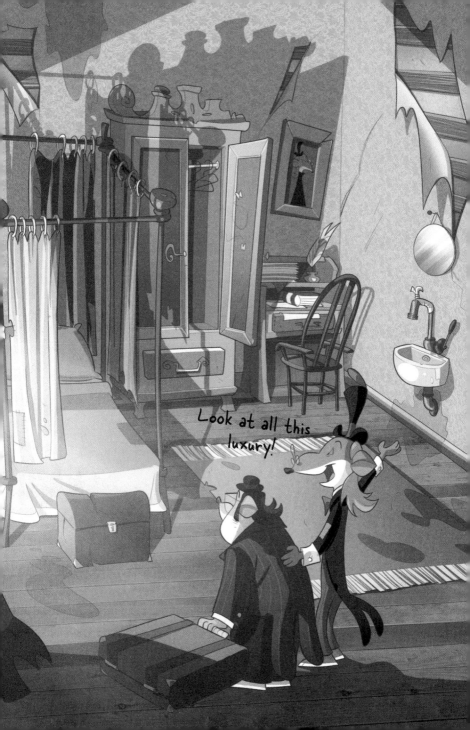

Hector looked around, sighing. He tried to sit on the bed, but it collapsed. He opened the drawer on the wardrobe, and a CLOUD OF TERMITES surrounded him. He turned on the rusty faucet in the corner sink, but only three drops of SMELLY SLIME came out.

Cough!

Yuck . . .

"RATS AND BATS!" exclaimed Hector. "So much for my rest. I should have never trusted the advertisement for this hotel. It is truly

falling to **pieces**. Oh well . . . I'm here now, so I may as well rehearse!"

He opened the enormouse suitcase. Inside, the ghosts of the circus snored *peacefully* in their jars.

Hector said loudly. "While you were all resting, I was **dragging** you all over this valley. But now it's your turn. We must begin rehearsals for tonight's show. Let's get moving!"

He opened the lid of every jar, and the performing ghosts **floated** out, happy to be free.

Meanwhile, on the floor below, Shamley and Lady Fifi were **bickering**.

"Transform the mansion into a hotel! Only

TUMBLING
GHOSTS

JUGGLING
PHANTOMS

STRONGMAN
GHOSTS

MAGICIAN
ECTOPLASM

ACROBATIC
PHANTOMS

CLOWN
GHOSTS

your moldy mind could come up with an idea like that!" Lady Fifi cried.

"This is a great idea," said Shamley. "Hector Spector travels all over. He can spread the word about how fine this place is!"

"AAAAAAAAAAAAHHHHHHH!"

A piercing scream echoed through the mansion, interrupting their argument.

THE MISSING GHOSTS

"What was that?" asked Lady Fifi.

"It came from the guest room!" exclaimed Shamley, RUNNING up the stairs.

He found Hector pacing the room, pulling at his whiskers.

"They're gone. Gone!" he wailed.

"Who?" asked Lady Fifi, GLANCING around the room. The dirty carpet was littered with open, EMPTY jars.

"The Prankster Ghosts!" Hector yelled. "Their jar is missing!"

He shook his head. "This is so strange. They always travel in the suitcase with the

other **GHOSTS**. Without them, I can't start rehearsal. I can't even have a show!"

Shamley looked around lazily. "Maybe they're somewhere **HERE** in the mansion."

Crash! Bang! Boom!

Lady Fifi turned pale.

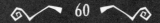

"That came from the CRYSTAL ROOM," she said.

The Crystal Room contained all the glasses, dishes, and platters in the mansion. The three rodents ran to the room — and found a TUMBLING GHOST practicing his routines. He was BREAKING every dish and cup in sight!

Lady Fifi saw the broken PIECES of her precious china and immediately fainted.

Shamley and Hector dragged her into the parlor and set her on a couch to recover.

A few minutes later, Lady Fifi opened an eye. Right at

that moment, a JUGGLING GHOST passed in front of her — and the objects he was juggling were her precious antique WIGS! She fainted again.

"I'm so sorry that my ghosts are misbehaving," said Hector. "Usually

Tra la la!

they are very polite, but since we can't practice without the Prankster Ghosts, I think they are **bored**."

Shamley was fanning his wife with his worn-out top hat. "You will understand that I must **raise** your rates for this!" he said.

At that moment, he felt a strange sensation. Something was lifting him up into the air! It was the **STRONGMAN GHOST**, who had picked him up as if he were as light as a feather. Now he **swung** Shamley around and around above his head.

"Forget it! I won't raise your rates!" Shamley yelled. "Just **LET ME DOWN** right now!"

But the ghost just spun him around more **quickly**.

"Okay! Okay! I'll give you a *discount*!" Shamley yelled.

The ghost tossed him in the air like a **cheese pizza**, catching him just inches before he hit the floor.

Whoa!

"Fine! You can stay for **FREE**!" Shamley yelled. "But, Hector, get these ghosts under control!"

GHOSTLY PRANKS

Not too far away, Creepella pulled her car in front of CACKLEFUR CASTLE. As soon as Creepella, Geronimo, Shivereen, and Bitewing came inside, they saw Boris von Cacklefur *pacing* in front of the entrance.

"It's a tragedy!" he cried, when he saw his daughter. "They glued them all together with chewing gum!"

"Oh no! What a DISASTER!" Creepella replied, immediately understanding her father.

"Who GLUED what?" Geronimo asked.

"Father's **COFFINS**, of course," Creepella replied.

"It will take a century to reopen them all!" Boris wailed. *"My whiskers will mold before I finish!"*

Suddenly they heard a clang from the dining room.

CRASH!

Oof!

Never in my career!

Creepella and Geronimo hurried into the dining room, where they found an **unusual** sight. Boneham, the perfectly PROPER butler of Cacklefur Castle, was sitting on the floor. Pieces of scattered BROKEN GLASS surrounded him.

"Miss Creepella!" moaned Boneham. "In my many years of service, I have never broken a thing! And now **LOOK**!"

"Holey cheese!" cried Geronimo. "How did this happen?"

Creepella pointed. "Don't you see? Someone substituted Boneham's shoes with **roller skates**!"

Then Shivereen ran in. "Auntie, please

come **right away**! Grandpa Frankenstein is very upset!"

Creepella and Geronimo followed Shivereen to the basement. Grandpa paced **nervously** back and forth, shaking his

My poor mummies!

Who was it?

Ooh . . .

paws. "They UNBANDAGED them, can you believe it? They unbandaged them one by one!

"Unbandaged what?" Geronimo asked.

"His MUMMIES, of course!" Creepella replied impatiently. "What else is bandaged around here?"

"Geronimo wants his mummy!" Bitewing teased, fluttering around the writer's head.

Creepella frowned. "This seems like an awful lot of tricks, even for the twins."

"Speaking of the twins, no one has SEEN them all morning," Shivereen told her. "Where could they have gone?"

"We are here . . . SIGH."

"Right here . . . sniff."

They all turned to see the twins sitting on the cellar stairs, crying. Creepella was about to scold them when she noticed something strange.

Someone had **TIED** the twins' tails together!

"Who did this?" she asked, astonished.

"We don't know," sniveled Snip.

"We were taking a nap," moaned Snap.

"And when we woke up . . ." continued Snip.

"We found our tails **TIED** together!" finished Snap.

Sniff!

Sigh!

The twins looked truly miserable.

"Well, I don't think that you two would have **tied** your own tails together," Creepella said. "So that means you probably haven't caused all the other **chaos** in the castle, either."

"So then who played all of these terrible **PRANKS**?" Geronimo asked.

"I don't have any idea . . . but I think we have a new **MYSTERY** on our paws!" exclaimed Creepella.

MISCHIEVOUS GHOST?

Creepella, Geronimo, Shivereen, and the WHIMPERING twins made their way back upstairs.

"Here is our mystery: Someone is PRANKING us behind our backs," she said. "And if it's not the twins, then who is it? Any idea, Gerrykins?"

"An INTRUDER?" Geronimo guessed.

"But what kind of intruder?" asked Creepella.

"A MUMMY come to life?" proposed Shivereen.

Geronimo's fur turned

PALE GREEN with fear.

"A monster that crawled out of the moat?" guessed Snip and Snap.

Now Geronimo was a **medium green,** like moldy cheese.

"Or maybe . . . a mischievous ghost?" Creepella suggested.

Geronimo turned **DARK GREEN**, like the deep forest.

Yikes!

"Gerrykins, do not even think about fainting right now!" warned Creepella. "You need to be clearheaded so we can begin our **SEARCH**."

"S-s-search?" Geronimo stammered.

"Yes! Whoever is pulling these pranks is **hidden** somewhere in the castle!" Creepella said.

"How do we proceed, Auntie?" Shivereen asked.

"We'll SPLiT UP," said Creepella. "Shivereen, you start in the Moldy Cellar."

Let's split up!

Creepella pointed to the twins. "Snip and Snap will stay on the first floor and keep watch while I check the bedrooms. Gerrykins, you must go to the top."

"What do you mean by the TOP?" Geronimo asked.

Creepella sighed. Geronimo was a great writer, but he didn't know much about Mysterious Valley. "This is a castle, Gerrykins. And every castle has t —"

"TERRACES?" Geronimo asked.

"No, to —"

"Toilets?" guessed Geronimo.

Creepella sighed her head. "No, I mean tow —"

"Towels?"

Creepella rolled her eyes, exasperated.

"Towers!" she told him.

"Oh, of course! TOWERS!" exclaimed

Geronimo. "But wait one minute. Do you mean that I have to go up there by myself to LOOK for a mummy or a monster or a ghost?"

Creepella nodded. "Yes! There is no time to lose!"

"R-r-r-right now?" Geronimo stammered.

"Yes, Geronimo," Creepella said. "Everyone, let's begin the search!" With trembling whiskers, Geronimo climbed up the first winding staircase

he saw, which led to **Bitewing's Tower.**
It seemed like it became NARROWER and
DARKER the higher he went.

Then Geronimo thought he heard a hiss.

"It's only my imagination," he muttered,
trying to give himself some COURAGE.

But then he heard another hiss — louder,
this time.

BAM!

A door slammed somewhere behind him.
Geronimo jumped. "Is someone there?"

Hiss . . . hiss . . . hiss . . .

The hisses were coming from behind him!
Heart **pounding**, he hurried up the last
steps as **quickly** as he could.

WHERE IS GERONIMO?

Creepella was discouraged. She had searched every inch of every bedroom but had not found anything **suspicious**. Shivereen had not found a single **CLUE** in the Moldy Cellar. And while they kept watch, Snip and Snap had seen only Boneham go by, with a **BANDAGED** bottom.

"Let's hope that Geronimo has found something," Creepella said. "It's been an hour since we began searching — plenty of time to check the towers. So **where is he?**"

Nobody had seen him.

"I hope he didn't get himself into some kind of **MESS**," Creepella said. "Snip and Snap, did you see which tower he went into?"

Over there! Over here!

"Um, over **THERE**," said Snip, pointing to stairs in the east wing.

"No, over **HERE**," said Snap, pointing to stairs in the west wing.

"I suppose I will have to *explore* them all, then," said Creepella, heading up the staircase to the Bewitched Tower. She didn't know that three pairs of **EYES** were following her.

"What do we do?"

"Do we *follow her*?"

"Yes, but don't let her see us!"

Milly, Tilly, and Lilly had arrived at

Cacklefur Castle to follow Geronimo. But when they had seen all the UNUSUAL PRANKS being played, they became curious. So they stayed hidden, hoping to catch the MYSTERIOUS prankster.

They followed Creepella up to the Bewitched Tower. It was filled with mirrors that created very strange reflections.

"Gerrykins!" called Creepella, but he didn't answer her. For a split second she thought she caught a glimpse of his reflection from the corner of her eye. She quickly turned around, but she didn't see him there.

"He isn't here," she muttered. "He must be in another tower."

As she left, the triplets stopped to check themselves out in the mirrors.

"This little HAT really looks great on

me!" bragged Tilly.

"But it's not as beautiful as mine!" said Milly.

Lilly sniffed. "I'm sorry for you both, but I am the **cutest**!"

While the Rattenbaums bickered, Creepella headed for Bitewing's Tower. To get there, she had to pass the Crocodile Pool and the **Piranha Tank**. She glanced at her fish. They seemed restless.

"What is it, little ones?" she asked.

The fish stared at her with their large round eyes, as if they wanted to say something.

"I'll check on you later," she said. "Now I must find that scaredy-mouse Geronimo!" Then she headed up the winding

staircase leading to the tower.

A few seconds later, the triplets entered the pool room.

"She came through here!"

"She went upstairs!"

"Keep following her!"

PRANKED AGAIN!

Creepella threw open the door of Bitewing's Tower. Her pet bat, along with all the other **BATS** in the castle, loved to sleep there during the day. They hung **upside down** from the rafters. Creepella saw many bats but not one newspaper mouse.

"Maybe Geronimo is in the watchtower," Creepella mused. As she turned to leave, her foot hit something: a **BUTT⊕N** from her friend's jacket.

"So Geronimo was here . . ."

"MMMMFF!"

Creepella thought she heard a muffled groan. She listened, and there it was again.

"**M**MMMFF!"

The sound came from a trunk in the middle of the room. Creepella opened it and saw . . .

"Gerrykins! Why are you in a TRUNK?"

"I — I don't know," he replied. He was CLUTCHING his knees to his chest and trembling. "I heard a sound coming from the trunk and when I bent down to look —"

"You got **pushed** in!" Creepella cried. "But why didn't you just push the lid open and get out?"

"I, um, knew I could do that, of course," Geronimo said. "I just wanted to, um,

inspect the trunk for **CLUES**!"

Creepella **smiled**. She knew her poor friend had been too scared to come out.

"And did you find any?" she asked.

"Er, no," Geronimo admitted.

Suddenly, three **LOUD** and terrible screams pierced their eardrums.

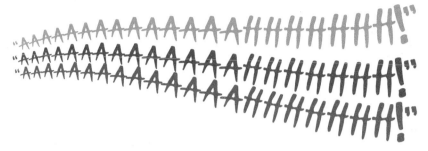

"Holey cheese!" Geronimo cried. "Who or what was that?"

Creepella grabbed him by the arm. "I know of only three creatures capable of SCREAMING like that. Come on!"

Dragging Geronimo against his will, Creepella went back downstairs to the pool room. As she had suspected, the Rattenbaum triplets were there. With their mouths open in HORROR, they were pointing at the Piranha Tank.

Three of the piranhas were wearing the triplets' hats! Creepella couldn't help herself and burst out laughing. The Rattenbaums got angry.

Ha, ha, h

"Easy for you to laugh!" said Tilly.

"Those **MONSTROUS** little beings didn't steal *your* hats!" added Milly.

"And throw them in the pool!" finished Lilly.

"**Little beings**, you said?" Creepella asked, suddenly curious. "What did they look like?"

"They were little!" said the first triplet.

"They were mushy!" said the second triplet.

"THEY WERE PALE!" said the third triplet.

"And they could fly!" all three finished at once.

"Very interesting," remarked Creepella. An idea was forming in her mind . . .

MYSTERY SOLVED!

The piranhas were starting to **nibble** on the triplets' hats when Shivereen walked in.

"What's going — **UH OH**! Be right back!" she exclaimed.

She rushed off and then appeared a minute later with a small toy **fishing rod**.

"I made this to fish out the fallen objects in the moat before **GORGO*** gobbles them," she explained. "I thought it might be useful now."

*Gorgo is the monster in Cacklefur Castle's moat. To get to know him, read Creepella's adventure *Meet Me in Horrorwood*.

Shivereen cleverly used the rod to fish the hats out of the Piranha Tank. The triplets put the soaked, chewed hats on their heads and went home, scowling. Creepella watched in silence as they left. She was very deep in thought.

"Creepella, is everything okay?" Geronimo asked timidly.

Creepella nodded. "Maybe. I'm close to solving the MYSTERY. Come with me!"

Geronimo and Shivereen followed her to her room, where she removed a heavy volume from her **bookshelf**: *The Daily Almanac of Mysterious Valley*. She leafed through it for a moment with a look of great concentration on her face. Then she let out a satisfied sigh.

"**HERE IT IS!**" she exclaimed.

Shivereen looked over her shoulder. "This

is the same description that the Rattenbaums gave of the P**R**A**NK**S**T**E**R**S!"

"Exactly!" exclaimed Creepella. "And did you see the last line?"

Shivereen nodded. "It's all coming together."

PRANKSTER GHOSTS

Very rare ghosts that come from the Laughing Mountain.

PERSONALITY: Although they like to hide from view, they are very cheerful and playful.

APPEARANCE: Small, mushy, and pale.

HABITAT: They are often found in circuses, where they invent funny routines.

"**What** are you two talking about?" asked Geronimo.

"Gerrykins, I don't have time to explain," said Creepella. "I must make a phone call!"

She quickly typed a number into her cell phone. After many rings, the Rattenbaums' elderly butler finally answered.

"Hello?"

"Hello, this is Creepella von Cackle —"

BOOM! The loud noise came through the phone.

"Excuse me," said the butler. "Things at the mansion are a little crazy today."

"Do Hector Spector's ghosts have anything to do with it?"

"Why, yes! They are causing quite a **panic**." the butler said.

BANG!

"May I please speak to your guest, **Hector Spector**?" Creepella replied.

"I'll call him right away!" the butler assured her.

After a long wait, she finally heard Hector's breathless voice on the other end.

"Creepella!" he cried. "This hotel is a disaster, my ghosts have **gone wild**, and even worse, I can't find —"

"The **PRANKSTER GHOSTS**?" she asked.

Hector was surprised.

"How did you know?"

"They are over here," Creepella replied. "We need to figure out **WHERE** they are and **HOW** they got here."

"I've been thinking," Hector said. "It's possible that someone got into my suitcase when I was sleeping next to that pear tree."

"Which pear tree?"

"Maybe it wasn't a pear tree," Hector said thoughtfully. "Maybe it was an apple tree . . . no, it was a WALNUT TREE!"

"A walnut tree. Hmm," Creepella said thoughtfully. "Please come over so we can get those ghosts."

"Right away!" said Hector.

Creepella ended the call. Now she had an idea of how those prankster ghosts had gotten into the castle.

"I must find SNiP and SNaP," she said.

HERE ARE THE GHOSTS!

Creepella found the twins with their tails still **TIED** together.

"If you don't tell me the truth right now, you won't get any **cheese** sandwiches for a month!" she threatened. "Did you take the Prankster Ghosts from Hector Spector?"

The twins looked at each other, frightened. They knew they could not lie to Creepella.

"We didn't know what was in the jar!" Snip blurted out. "When we opened it, it seemed EMPTY!"

"Then we were tired, so we went to

sleep," Snap added.

"We were tired because we woke up extra early to —" Snip began, but a nudge from his brother stopped him.

Geronimo had finally figured out what had happened. "If you let the ghosts out, then you must get them back," he said.

"That will not be easy!" said Hector Spector, bursting into the castle at just that moment. "These ghosts love to play TRICKS, and it sounds like they have been having a good time here."

"Is there some way we can lure them back in the jar?" Shivereen asked.

Hector sighed. "I don't know."

Then Madame LaTomb walked in. "Good day — ACHOO! I'm finally feeling better.

Did something *happen* while I was sick?" she asked.

Before anyone could reply, Chef Stewrat came in holding a bowl of very **stinky** stew.

"Madame! What are you doing?" he asked her. "I have brought you my Feel Better Stew! It can cure the common cold, or a **tarantula's** headache, an **earthworm's** stiff neck, or a ghost's allergies."

As soon as he said the word *ghost*, Madame LaTomb's hair began to rustle. It was not HOWLER, her were-canary. Instead, three little pale, mushy ghosts popped up, sniffing the stinky stew.

"MY DEAR GHOSTS!"

exclaimed Hector happily.

"Even they can't resist Chef Stewrat's stew," remarked Creepella, amused.

Hector gently scolded the phantoms. "Enough PRANKS, please. The von Cacklefur family has been very **patient** with you. But now it is time to go. The others have been waiting for you for hours, and we must begin rehearsals for the **SHOW**!"

The three Prankster Ghosts **happily** fluttered back to Hector Spector, glad to have found their friend. They **floated** right into the jar, ready to be taken to Rattenbaum Mansion and to prepare for the big show.

Hi, Hector!

Here we are!

THE GALLOPING
GHOST CIRCUS

"Dear Creepella, how can I thank you?" asked a very relieved Hector Spector.

"Well, there is that **interview** you promised me. May we do it now?" she asked.

"Of course!" Hector replied. "And you and your whole family are invited to the show tonight so that you can forgive me for the trouble I've caused you."

Shivereen clapped her hands and cheered. "HOORAY!"

"Can we come, too?" asked Snip and Snap timidly.

Creepella stared at the twins, thinking.

They seemed to be **sorry**, and their poor tails were still tied together.

"Yes, you may come," she replied. "But first you must apologize to Mr. Spector and **help** him with his rehearsals. Gerrykins, untie their tails!"

While Geronimo went to work, they all heard a noise on the stairs. Howler was hopping down them, step by step. He was in a terrible mood.

"It is **UNACCEPTABLE! UNHEARD OF! RIDICULOUS!**" he shrieked. "Me, the most **FEROCIOUS** were-canary in Mysterious Valley, evicted from my nest by three silly little ghosts. **Sheesh!**"

Sheesh!

Everyone laughed.

The mysterious adventure was over!

That night, they all gathered

under the big tent to witness the most **EXCITING**, **MONSTROUS**, and **UNPREDICTABLE** show ever seen in Gloomeria:

THE GALLOPING GHOST CIRCUS!

A Great Success!

As soon as I finished reading the story, a great coMmotion sprung up around me and Benjamin.

CLAP CLAP CLAP

The other rodents in line to buy tickets for the circus were applauding. They all loved Creepella's latest tale!

"What a thrilling story indeed, Mr. Stilton," remarked a mouse in front of me. "Very strange and spooky."

"Of course, you did seem like a bit of a scaredy-mouse," added another rodent.

The rodent next to him agreed. "Yes, a scaredy-mouse!"

"But you must **publish** this story!" someone else added, and everyone in line agreed.

"It's sensational!" "EXCITING AND FRIGHTENING!"

"Did you hear that, Uncle?" asked Benjamin. "Everyone wants you to publish it. You have a bestseller in your paws."

I nodded. Creepella had done it again! That didn't surprise me. She is the most TERRIFYING author of thrilling tales in all of Mysterious Valley!

Then the line started to move quickly.

Editing Creepella's book would have to wait until tomorrow. Nothing could keep me from seeing the FLYING FUR CIRCUS!

"What do you think, Uncle?" asked Benjamin. "Do you think it will be as good as Hector Spector's Galloping Ghost Circus?"

"Well, it might not be quite as **spooktacular**, but I'm sure it will be spectacular," I replied with a grin. "We will have a good time, or my name isn't Stilton, *Geronimo Stilton*!"

Don't miss any of my thrilling tales!

#1 THE THIRTEEN GHOSTS

#2 MEET ME IN HORRORWOOD

#3 GHOST PIRATE TREASURE

#4 RETURN OF THE VAMPIRE

#5 FRIGHT NIGHT

#6 RIDE FOR YOUR LIFE!

#7 A SUITCASE FULL OF GHOSTS

Be sure to read all my fabumouse adventures!

#1 Lost Treasure of the Emerald Eye

#2 The Curse of the Cheese Pyramid

#3 Cat and Mouse in a Haunted House

#4 I'm Too Fond of My Fur!

#5 Four Mice Deep in the Jungle

#6 Paws Off, Cheddarface!

#7 Red Pizzas for a Blue Count

#8 Attack of the Bandit Cats

#9 A Fabumouse Vacation for Geronimo

#10 All Because of a Cup of Coffee

#11 It's Halloween, You 'Fraidy Mouse!

#12 Merry Christmas, Geronimo!

#13 The Phantom of the Subway

#14 The Temple of the Ruby of Fire

#15 The Mona Mousa Code

#16 A Cheese-Colored Camper

#17 Watch Your Whiskers, Stilton!

#18 Shipwreck on the Pirate Islands

#19 My Name Is Stilton, Geronimo Stilton

#20 Surf's Up, Geronimo!

#21 The Wild, Wild West

#22 The Secret of Cacklefur Castle

A Christmas Tale

#23 Valentine's Day Disaster

#24 Field Trip to Niagara Falls

#25 The Search for Sunken Treasure

#26 The Mummy with No Name

#27 The Christmas Toy Factory

#28 Wedding Crasher

#29 Down and Out Down Under

#30 The Mouse Island Marathon

#31 The Mysterious Cheese Thief

Christmas Catastrophe

#32 Valley of the Giant Skeletons

#33 Geronimo and the Gold Medal Mystery

#34 Geronimo Stilton, Secret Agent

#35 A Very Merry Christmas

#36 Geronimo's Valentine

#37 The Race Across America

#38 A Fabumouse School Adventure

#39 Singing Sensation

#40 The Karate Mouse

#41 Mighty Mount Kilimanjaro

#42 The Peculiar Pumpkin Thief

#43 I'm Not a Supermouse!

#44 The Giant Diamond Robbery

#45 Save the White Whale!

#46 The Haunted Castle

#47 Run for the Hills, Geronimo!

#48 The Mystery in Venice

#49 The Way of the Samurai

#50 This Hotel Is Haunted!

#51 The Enormouse Pearl Heist

#52 Mouse in Space!

#53 Rumble in the Jungle

#54 Get into Gear, Stilton!

#55 The Golden Statue Plot

#56 Flight of the Red Bandit

The Hunt for the Golden Book

#57 The Stinky Cheese Vacation

#58 The Super Chef Contest

#59 Welcome to Moldy Manor

The Hunt for the Curious Cheese

#60 The Treasure of Easter Island

Don't miss my journeys through time!

Meet
GERONIMO STILTONOOT

He is a cavemouse—Geronimo Stilton's ancient ancestor! He runs the stone newspaper in the prehistoric village of Old Mouse City. From dealing with dinosaurs to dodging meteorites, his life in the Stone Age is full of adventure!

#1 The Stone of Fire

#2 Watch Your Tail!

#3 Help, I'm in Hot Lava!

#4 The Fast and the Frozen

#5 The Great Mouse Race

#6 Don't Wake the Dinosaur!

#7 I'm a Scaredy-Mouse!

#8 Surfing for Secrets

Be sure to check out these exciting adventures from my sister, Thea Stilton!

Thea Stilton and the Dragon's Code

Thea Stilton and the Mountain of Fire

Thea Stilton and the Ghost of the Shipwreck

Thea Stilton and the Secret City

Thea Stilton and the Mystery in Paris

Thea Stilton and the Cherry Blossom Adventure

Thea Stilton and the Star Castaways

Thea Stilton: Big Trouble in the Big Apple

Thea Stilton and the Ice Treasure

Thea Stilton and the Secret of the Old Castle

Thea Stilton and the Blue Scarab Hunt

Thea Stilton and the Prince's Emerald

Thea Stilton and the Mystery on the Orient Express

Thea Stilton and the Dancing Shadows

Thea Stilton and the Legend of the Fire Flowers

Thea Stilton and the Spanish Dance Mission

Thea Stilton and the Journey to the Lion's Den

Thea Stilton and the Great Tulip Heist

Thea Stilton and the Chocolate Sabotage

Thea Stilton and the Missing Myth

1. Mountains of the Mangy Yeti
2. Cacklefur Castle
3. Angry Walnut Tree
4. Rattenbaum Mansion
5. Rancidrat River
6. Bridge of Shaky Steps
7. Squeakspeare Mansion
8. Slimy Swamp
9. Ogre Highway
10. Gloomeria
11. Shivery Arts Academy
12. Horrorwood Studios

CACKLEFUR CASTLE

1. Oozing moat

2. Drawbridge

3. Grand entrance

4. Moldy basement

5. Patio, with a view of the moat

6. Dusty library

7. Room for unwanted guests

8. Mummy room

9. Watchtower

10. Creaking staircase

11. Banquet room

12. Garage (for antique hearses)

13. Bewitched tower

14. Garden of carnivorous plants

15. Stinky kitchen

16. Crocodile pool and piranha tank

17. Creepella's room

18. Tower of musky tarantulas

19. Bitewing's tower (with antique contraptions)

DEAR MOUSE FRIENDS, GOOD-BYE UNTIL THE NEXT BOOK!